The
Puddleman

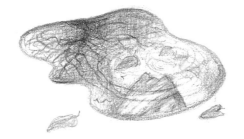

The
Puddleman

RAYMOND BRIGGS

JONATHAN CAPE
London

For
CONNIE MATILDA & MILES

The Puddleman
A Jonathan Cape Book 0 224 07009 6

Published in Great Britain by Jonathan Cape,
an imprint of Random House Children's Books

This edition published 2004

1 3 5 7 9 10 8 6 4 2

RANDOM HOUSE CHILDREN'S BOOKS
61-63 Uxbridge Road, London W5 5SA
A division of The Random House Group Ltd
RANDOM HOUSE AUSTRALIA (PTY) LTD
20 Alfred Street, Milsons Point, Sydney,
New South Wales 2061, Australia
RANDOM HOUSE NEW ZEALAND LTD
18 Poland Road, Glenfield, Auckland 10, New Zealand
RANDOM HOUSE (PTY) LTD
Endulini, 5A Jubilee Road, Parktown 2193, South Africa

THE RANDOM HOUSE GROUP Limited Reg. No. 954009
www.kidsatrandomhouse.co.uk

A CIP catalogue record for this book is available from the British Library.

Printed and bound in Singapore

We've all gone away.

Would you like to give me a hand?

Yes, but I've got Collar
on a lead.

Is that your dog?

No.
It's my grandfather.

Oh, an old boy like that
can look after himself.

Are they puddles
on your back?

Yes, that's right.
There's all different sizes
of puddles nowadays.
They have to fit the hollows
in the ground, see?

Have you got the
big, yellowy one?

Oh, yes. I know the one you mean.
If you like, we'll do that one first.
I'll be pleased to be rid of it.
It's far and away the heaviest one.

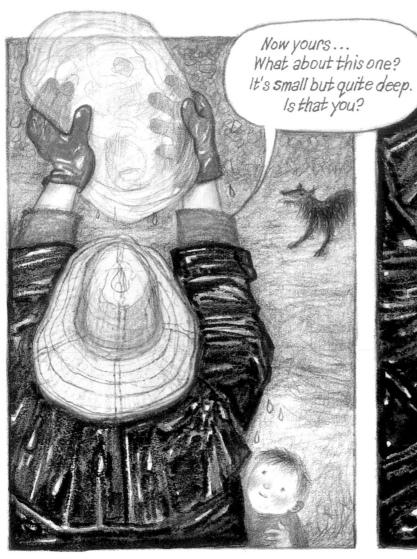

So they went home to Grannie's house for a tea of beans on toast with black and trees.

THE END

With grateful acknowledgements to MILES for
The naming of puddles
Collar
I think... I THINK this one... MIGHT be Auntie Clare
Black
They haven't put any puddle in that one
Trees
Silly!